The
Princess
Knight

First published in Germany by Fischer Taschenbuch Verlag GmbH © 2001

This paperback edition first published in the United Kingdom in 2004 by
The Chicken House, 2 Palmer Street, Frome, Somerset, BA11 1DS
www.doublecluck.com

Text © 2001 Cornelia Funke
Illustrations © 2001 Kerstin Meyer
English translation © 2003 Anthea Bell

Printed and bound in Italy

British Library Cataloguing in Publication Data available

ISBN: 1 904442 14 5

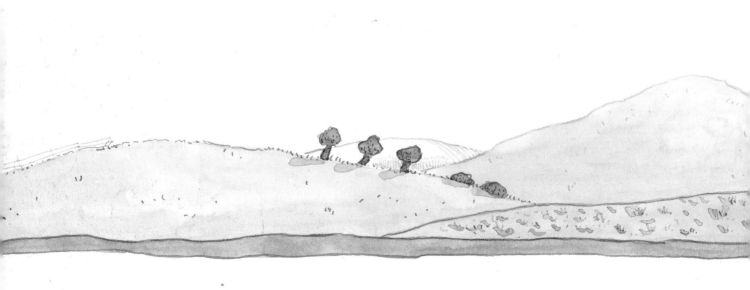

The Princess Knight

By
Cornelia Funke

Illustrations by
Kerstin Meyer

The Chicken House

King Wilfred the Worthy had three sons.
He brought them up just as his father had brought *him* up,
and they were taught all the things *he* had been taught.

They learned riding and jousting, fighting with swords and good table manners.

They learned how to stride around proudly and how to shout *very* loudly.

And (most important for princes) they learned how to give orders – to their nursemaids, their servants, their dogs and their horses.

Then Queen Violetta had a daughter
but died when the baby was born.

No one would dare tell the king *how* to do anything –
especially how to raise his little girl. So he called her Violetta
and decided to teach her the same lessons as he had taught
his sons . . .

. . . even though she was so small she could hardly
lift a sword at all!

Her brothers teased her and called her names.
'Itsy-Bitsy Little Vi –
Tiny-titch can't hurt a fly!'

And they would boast that they could
dig their spurs into a horse so hard
that even the most spirited steed
would obey them.

Then they'd strike the heads off the practice dummies
so hard that they would fly right over the castle walls.

And they would laugh and laugh at their little sister
as she struggled to mount a horse in her heavy armour,
as if it was the funniest thing they'd ever seen.

'Oh, Emma,' said Violetta to her maid one evening, when Emma was soothing her poor bruises. 'I'll never be as strong as my brothers.'

'Not as strong, maybe, but you are three times as clever,' said Emma sensibly. 'Why not ask your father to let you stop all this silly fighting and learn something else? Embroidery perhaps. Or weaving. Or playing the flute. Something really *useful?*'

But Violetta shook her head.

'No, no, no,' she said. 'That would only make my brothers laugh louder.'

So Emma said no more. For she knew her princess was more determined than all the three princes put together.

From that night onwards, Violetta slipped out of the castle in secret, while the rose gardener's son kept watch for her.

She started to practise all the things her brothers could already do so much better.

Violetta practised them in her own way,
without shouting and without using her spurs.

She was very quiet about it: as quiet as the night itself.

So, while her brothers grew as tall and strong as King Wilfred's knights, Violetta got better at fighting and riding every day. And her father's horses loved to carry her on their backs.

Violetta was so nimble and quick that when the three
brothers practised jousting with her, their spears and swords
just hit the empty air. And the princes soon stopped
laughing at her and calling her 'Itsy-Bitsy Little Vi!'

But then came the day before her sixteenth birthday
and the king asked to see her.

'Violetta,' said King Wilfred, 'I'm going to hold a tournament
in honour of your birthday. The victory prize will bring the
bravest knights in the land flocking to the castle.'

'What will the prize be, Father?' asked Violetta, wondering
which horse to ride, which of her suits of armour would be
lightest, and what plume to wear in her helmet.

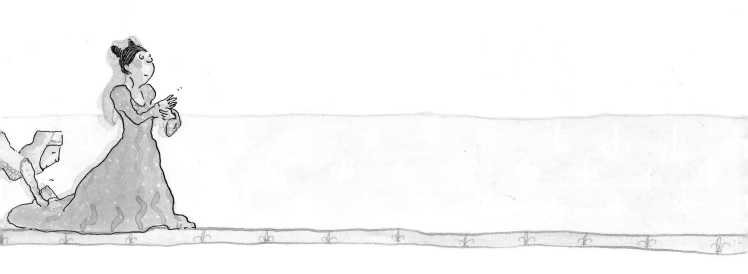

'The prize,' said King Wilfred, 'will be your hand in marriage. So put on your finest gown and practise your prettiest smile.'

Violetta went as red as the poppies beside the castle moat.

'What!' she cried. You want *me* to marry some idiot in a tin suit? Just look at your own knights! They whip their horses and are too stupid to write their own names!'

Her father was so angry that he locked her up in the castle tower with the rats and the bats. Not until the moon was shining high in the sky did he tell Violetta's youngest brother to let her out.

'Stop crying, little sister!' said Violetta's brother. 'I'm going to win the tournament, and you can't marry me!'

But Violetta shook her head and wiped her eyes on the hem of her dress.

'Thank you,' she said, 'but I think I'd better just see to it myself.'

The next day was Violetta's birthday. The field behind the
castle was crowded with knights who had come to fight in the
tournament. King Wilfred sat down to watch. Little did he know
that it wasn't Violetta sitting beside him. It was her maid Emma,

wearing Violetta's best dress and with a veil drawn over her face.
    The real Violetta put on her blackest armour and saddled her
favourite horse. She rode into the arena with the other knights
and gave her title as 'Sir No-Name.'

Fanfares sounded and the tournament to win the princess's hand began. Knight after knight rode into the arena – Sigurd the Strong, Harold the Hardy, Percy the Pitiless – but Sir No-Name defeated them all. He even knocked the king's sons off their horses and into the dust.

In the end there was no one left willing to fight.
And Sir No-Name rode over to the king
to receive the Victor's Wreath.

'Where do you come from, Sir No-Name?' asked the king.
'You have brought honour to your family, and my daughter
should think herself lucky to take your hand in marriage.'

'Oh, I don't think so!' the knight replied, raising his helmet . . .

'Hello Father,' said Violetta. 'What's the prize for a *Princess* Knight?'

And for once in his life, her father the king was speechless.

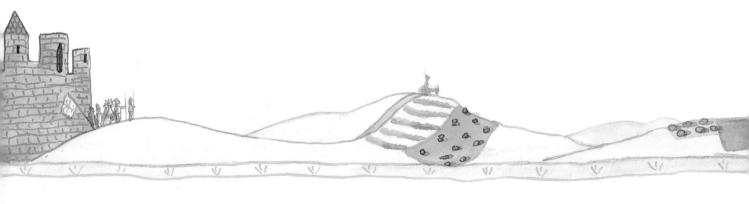

Violetta turned to the vanquished knights, sitting battered
and bruised on their horses.

'Very well, I shall choose my own prize,' she said. . .

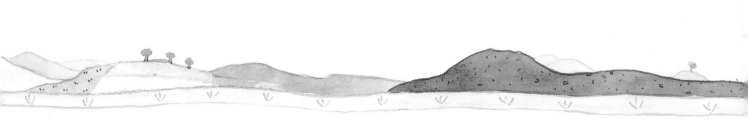

. . .'I hereby proclaim that no one will ever win the Princess
Violetta's hand in marriage without first defeating Sir No-Name.'

Then she turned her horse and rode away – far, far away.
And she didn't return for a year and a day.

And when she did? Why, her father, King Wilfred the Worthy,
gave her a horse – as black as her armour. And nobody, not even her
brothers, challenged the princess ever again.

And who *did* she marry? Well, if you must know, many years
later, she married the rose gardener's son and lived happily ever after.

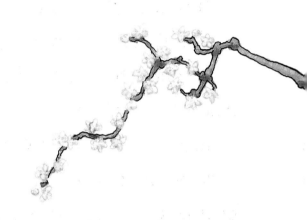

Born in Dorsten, Germany in 1958, *Cornelia Funke* is the author of the international best-seller *The Thief Lord* published by The Chicken House in 2002, and Inkheart published in 2003. She has been writing and illustrating childrens books since 1987 and now lives with her husband and two children in Hamburg, Germany.

Kerstin Meyer was born in Wedel near Hamburg in 1966.
She studied illustration at Hamburg College of Design.
Since taking her diploma in 1993 she has worked as an illustrator for several publishers of children's books as well as for television.